SPACE WORDS
A DICTIONARY

SEYMOUR SIMON
SPACE WORDS
A DICTIONARY

illustrated by RANDY CHEWNING

HarperCollins*Publishers*

The illustrations in this book were drawn with
pen and ink and painted with watercolors.
The skies were painted with an airbrush.

Space Words: A Dictionary
Text copyright © 1991 by Seymour Simon
Illustrations copyright © 1991 by Randy Chewning
Printed in Mexico. All rights reserved.
2 3 4 5 6 7 8 9 10

Library of Congress Cataloging-in-Publication Data
Simon, Seymour.
    Space words : a dictionary / by Seymour Simon ; illustrated
by Randy Chewning.
        p.   cm.
    Summary: Defines words and terms commonly used in
discussing outer space—from Apollo Program to Zodiac.
    ISBN 0-06-022532-7. — ISBN 0-06-022533-5 (lib. bdg.)
    1. Outer space—Dictionaries, Juvenile.   2. Astronomy—
Dictionaries, Juvenile.   3. Astronautics—Dictionaries,
Juvenile.   [1. Outer space—Dictionaries.   2. Astronomy—
Dictionaries.   3. Astronautics—Dictionaries.]   I. Chewning,
Randy, ill.   II. Title.
QB497.S55   1991   90-37402
500.5′03—dc20   CIP
                                                              AC

To the Hayden Planetarium, where I spent some
of the happiest hours of my youth
—S.S.

To Anne
—R.C.

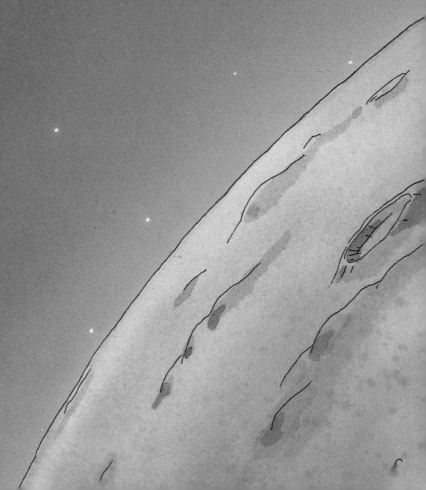

***Apollo* Program** A United States space program whose purpose was to land men on the moon. There were 17 *Apollo* missions, and 6 made lunar (moon) landings. On July 20, 1969, *Apollo 11* astronaut Neil Armstrong became the first person to set foot on the moon.

astronaut A space traveler. An astronaut is specially trained to fly in a spaceship and work in space. The word used in the Soviet Union is cosmonaut.

asteroid One of the millions of small, rocky bodies that orbit the sun. Most asteroids revolve (circle) around the sun in a ring, or "asteroid belt," between the orbits of Mars and Jupiter.

astronomy The scientific study of stars, planets, comets, asteroids, galaxies, quasars, pulsars, black holes, and all the other natural phenomena beyond Earth.

atmosphere   The layer of gases that surrounds a planet. Earth has an atmosphere made up mostly of the gases nitrogen and oxygen.

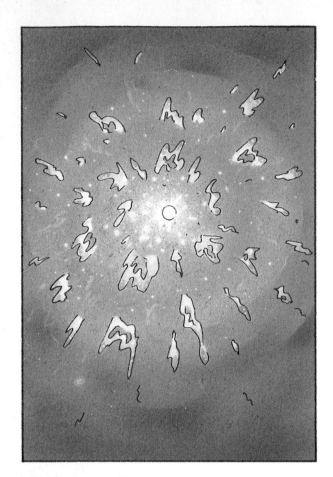

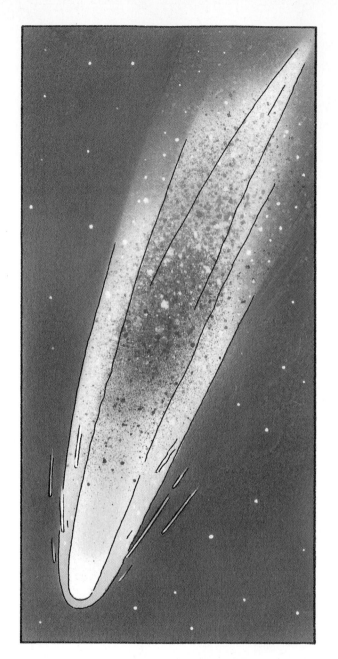

big bang theory A theory about the beginning of the universe. The big bang theory says that the universe began about 15 to 20 billion years ago with an explosion of a great, hot ball of matter. The universe expanded in all directions; the matter began to cool and formed stars and galaxies.

black hole A place in space with enormous gravity. It is called a black hole because nothing, not even light, can escape from it. A black hole can result from the collapse of a supergiant star.

comet A lump of dust and ice left over when the solar system formed. Some astronomers call comets "dirty snowballs." When a comet comes near the sun, it grows a glowing head and tail and begins to shine.

constellation A group of bright stars that form a shape or pattern in the sky. The ancient stargazers named the constellations after creatures or objects they thought the shapes resembled. The stars in a constellation are seldom close to each other in space—they only appear to be.

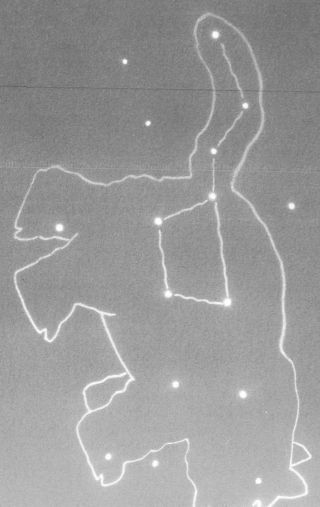

Ursa Minor (Little Bear)

Ursa Major (Big Bear)

Copernicus, Nicolaus (1473–1543) A Polish astronomer who proposed the idea that the sun was the center of the universe. Before that, most people thought Earth was the center of the universe.

cosmic rays Tiny high-energy particles that bombard Earth from outer space. When cosmic rays hit Earth's atmosphere, they produce harmless, low-energy particles.

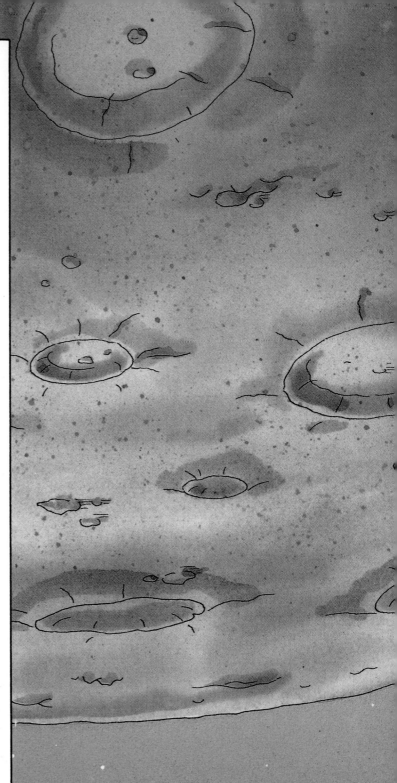

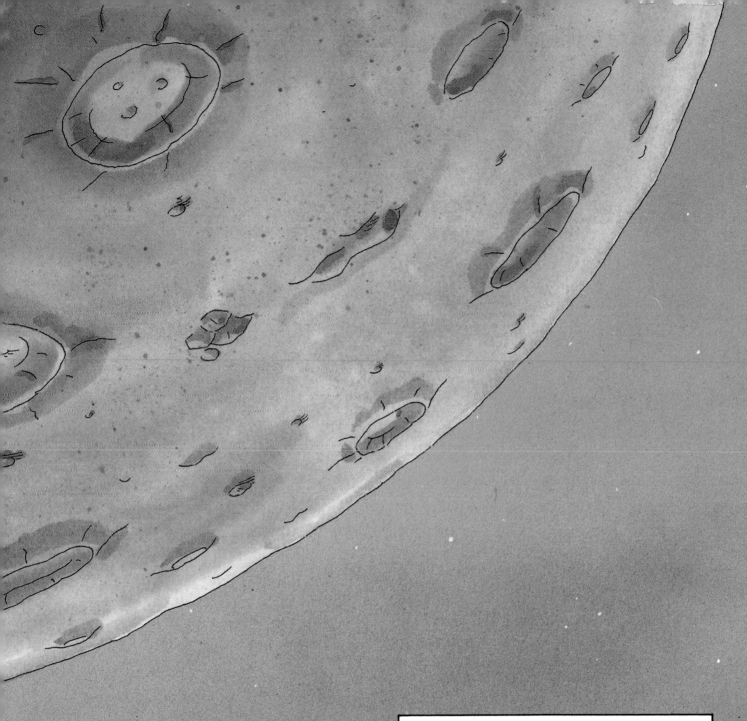

crater A circular hollow in the surface of a planet or moon. Most craters are formed when a rock crashes into the ground from outer space.

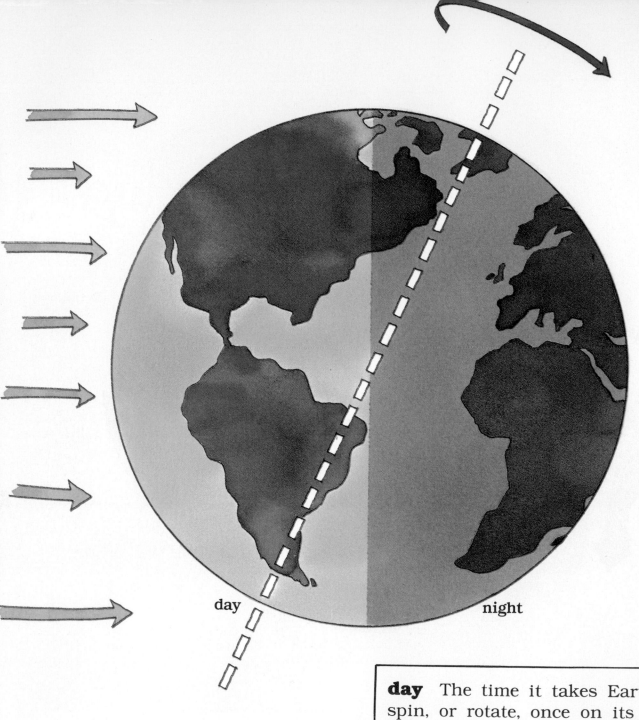

day   night

day The time it takes Earth to spin, or rotate, once on its axis. When measured in relation to the stars, a day on Earth is about 23 hours 56 minutes 4 seconds. When measured in relation to the sun, a day is 24 hours.

double star   A pair of stars that appear close together in the sky. Some double stars, called binaries, really are near each other in space and travel around a common center of gravity. About half of all stars are either binaries or belong to larger star groups.

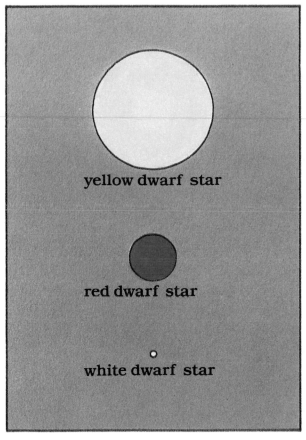

yellow dwarf star

red dwarf star

white dwarf star

dwarf star   Our sun is a medium-sized yellow dwarf star. Red dwarf stars are smaller and dimmer than yellow dwarfs. White dwarf stars are even smaller—they are slowly cooling down and are near the ends of their lives.

Earth   The rocky, watery planet on which we live. Earth is the third planet from the sun, about 93 million miles (150 million kilometers) away. The diameter at the equator is 7,926 miles (12,756 kilometers), about 26 miles (43 kilometers) more than at the poles. Earth is the only body in the solar system that has all the materials and conditions needed for life as we know it.

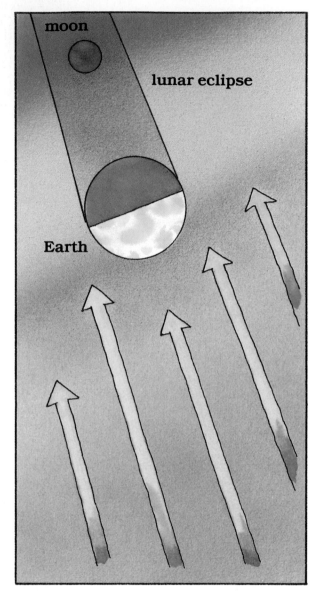

moon

lunar eclipse

Earth

eclipse When one body in space blocks our view of another body in space. A total eclipse blocks the entire body; a partial eclipse blocks only part of it. When the moon passes in front of the sun, we have a solar (sun) eclipse. When the moon passes into Earth's shadow, we have a lunar (moon) eclipse.

Einstein, Albert (1879–1955) A German-born Swiss-American physicist who changed our ideas of space, time, gravity, and the universe with his theories of relativity. He is best known for his formula $E=mc^2$ (energy is equal to mass multiplied by the square of the speed of light), which helps explain the energy of the sun and stars.

equinox One of the two times during the year when day and night are of equal length all over the world. The spring, or vernal, equinox happens on about March 21, and the autumnal equinox happens on about September 23.

Explorer 1 The first United States satellite. The 31-pound (14-kilogram) satellite was launched on January 31, 1958. It remained in orbit for more than 12 years, traveling nearly 60 thousand times around Earth.

extraterrestrial life Living things from other worlds. The search for extraterrestrial life has so far been unsuccessful.

falling star *See* meteor

galaxy A huge system of stars, nebulas, dust, and gases. Millions of galaxies have been discovered in distant space. A galaxy may contain hundreds of thousands of millions of stars moving through space together.

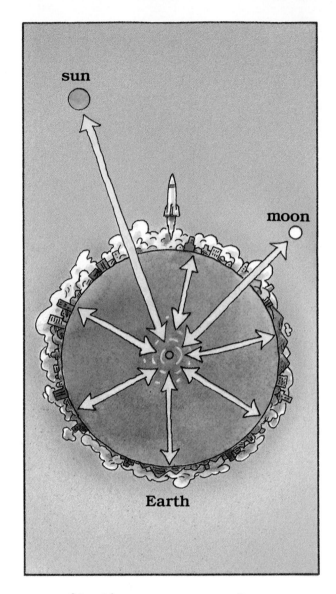

Galilei, Galileo (1564–1642) An Italian astronomer and physicist who made the first telescopic observations of the night sky. He discovered the rings of Saturn, the four largest moons of Jupiter, the phases of Venus, and the fact that the sun turns. His observations led him to support Copernicus's theory that the sun is the center of the universe.

gravitation or gravity The invisible force of attraction that exists between all matter. The gravitational attraction of the sun keeps the planets from whirling off into space. Gravitation holds a star together. It attracts you to the center of Earth and gives you weight. Gravitation is one of the basic forces in the universe.

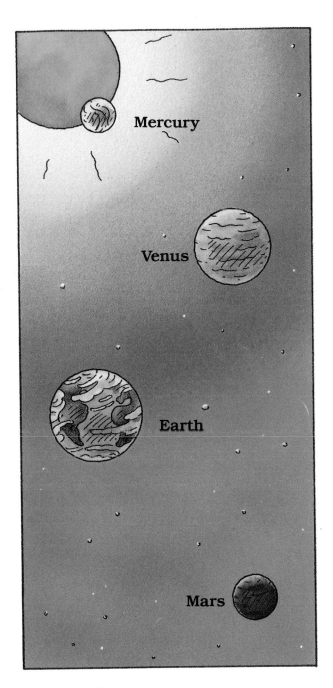

Halley's comet   A famous comet named after Edmund Halley (1656–1742), who first determined its 76-year-long orbit. It was last seen without a telescope in 1986.

inner planets   Mercury, Venus, Earth, and Mars. These four small, rocky planets are closer to the sun than the four giant outer planets, Jupiter, Saturn, Uranus, and Neptune, and the tiny icy planet Pluto.

21

Jupiter By far the largest planet in the solar system, twice the size of all the other planets put together. Jupiter is a gas giant, about 88 thousand miles (143 thousand kilometers) across, and orbits about 480 million miles (780 million kilometers) from the sun. Jupiter has faint rings and at least 16 moons.

Kepler, Johannes (1571–1630) A German astronomer whose laws of motion helped scientists to understand how planets move.

light year A basic unit used to measure great distances in space. It is the distance light travels in one year, about 5.9 million million (5,900,000,000,000) miles (9.5 million million kilometers).

lunar eclipse *See* eclipse

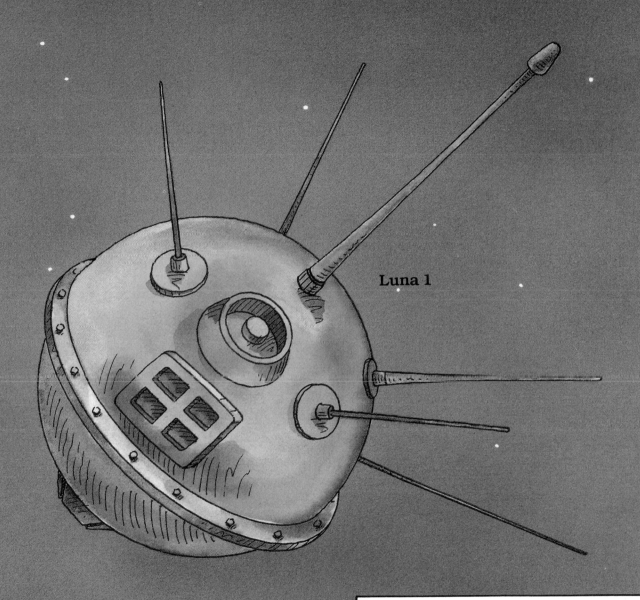

Luna 1

Luna A series of unmanned Russian spacecraft sent to explore the moon. In 1959 *Luna 2* was the first probe ever to reach the moon. In 1970 a capsule from *Luna 16* returned to Earth with a sample of soil from the surface of the moon.

Magellanic Clouds The two galaxies nearest to our Milky Way galaxy. Each is much smaller than the Milky Way.

magnitude A measure of a star's brightness. Very bright stars are given a magnitude of 1. The faintest stars visible to the unaided eye are given a magnitude of 6. The largest telescopes have photographed stars of magnitude 26.

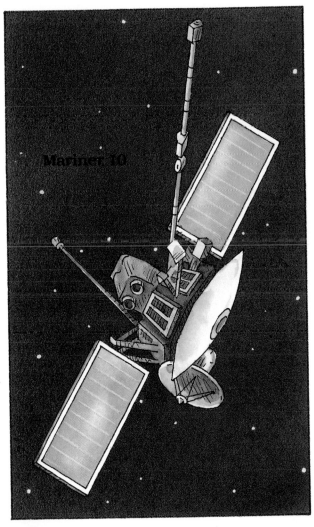

Mariner A series of United States space probes sent to study the nearest planets—Venus, Mars, and Mercury.

Mars The fourth planet from the sun. It is about 4,220 miles (6,790 kilometers) across and is about 142 million miles (228 million kilometers) from the sun. Mars goes around the sun once in 687 (Earth) days. A day on Mars is about 40 minutes longer than a day on Earth. Mars has a thin atmosphere of mostly carbon dioxide and is much colder than Earth. As far as we know, no life exists on Mars.

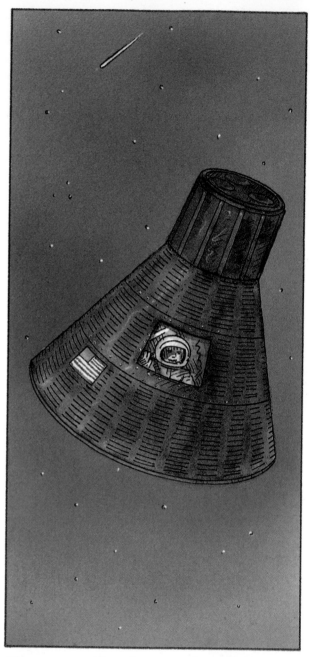

Mercury The planet closest to the sun. Mercury is about 36 million miles (58 million kilometers) away from the sun. Mercury is a hot, lifeless ball of rock about 3,015 miles (4,850 kilometers) across, the second-smallest planet after Pluto. The cratered surface of Mercury looks much like that of the moon.

***Mercury* Project** The first United States program to launch men into space. On February 20, 1962, *Mercury* astronaut John Glenn became the first American to go into orbit.

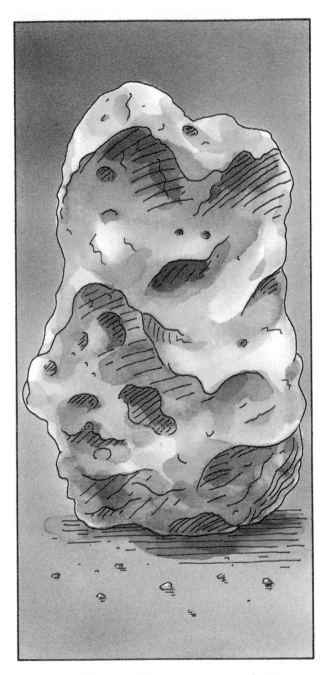

meteor The streak of light seen in the night sky when a particle or rock from space, called a meteoroid, plunges through Earth's atmosphere and burns up because of friction. A meteor is sometimes called a falling or shooting star, although it is not a star.

meteorite The remains of a large meteoroid that was not completely burned up when it fell through Earth's atmosphere. Meteorites are made of rock, metal, or both substances.

27

Milky Way The white band of light from many stars that arcs across the night sky. It is what we see from Earth when we look out at the Milky Way galaxy.

Milky Way galaxy The large group of stars that includes our sun. All the stars you see in the night sky are in the Milky Way galaxy. Also called just the Galaxy.

mission control The group of people who direct and take charge of a space flight.

Moon Earth's nearest neighbor in space. The moon is about 239 thousand miles (384 thousand kilometers) away. It is about 2,160 miles (3,476 kilometers) across. If Earth were hollow, 50 moons could fit inside. The moon is an airless, waterless, lifeless place of mountains, craters, and broad lava plains. Because of the moon's low gravity, on the surface of the moon you would weigh only about one sixth your weight on Earth. The moon revolves around Earth once every 27 days and 8 hours. It always keeps the same side facing toward us. (*See also* phases of the moon.)

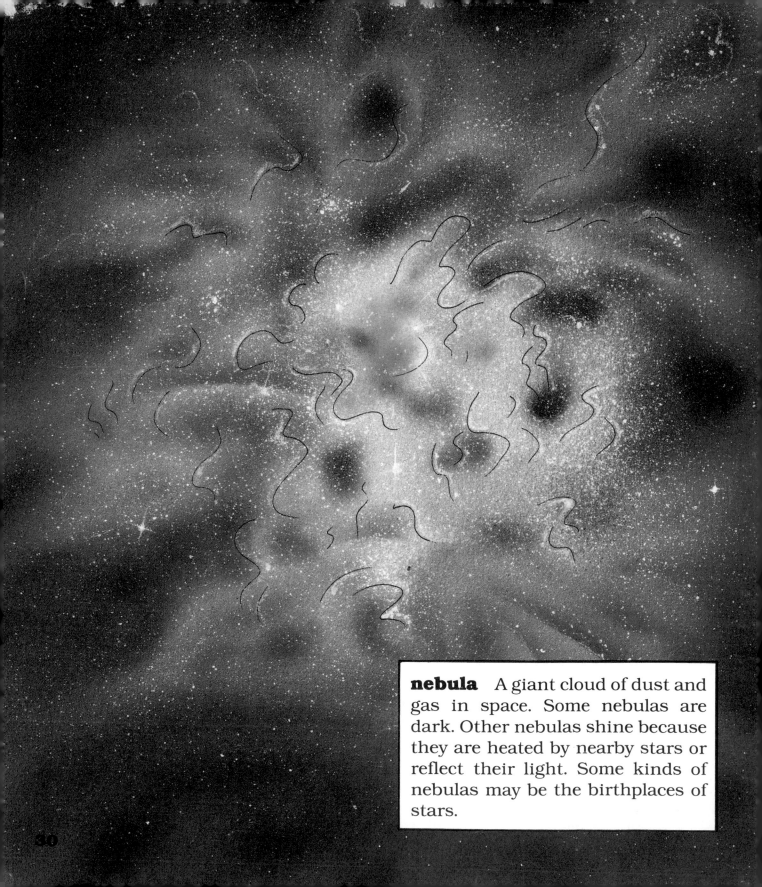

nebula A giant cloud of dust and gas in space. Some nebulas are dark. Other nebulas shine because they are heated by nearby stars or reflect their light. Some kinds of nebulas may be the birthplaces of stars.

Neptune   The fourth-largest planet in the solar system. Neptune is about 31 thousand miles (50 thousand kilometers) across. It is now the most distant planet, on average 28 thousand million miles (45 thousand million kilometers) from the sun. Pluto will become the most distant planet again in 1999. This occurs because of Pluto's odd path around the sun, which sometimes brings it within the orbit of Neptune.

sun

New York

○ neutron star

neutron star   The densely packed remains of a collapsed giant star. A neutron star may be only about the size of New York or London, yet contain more matter than the sun.

Newton, Sir Isaac (1642–1726)
An English scientist and mathematician who is the author of the theory of universal gravitation—that every body in the universe attracts every other body. He also formulated the three laws of motion, which apply as much to the fall of an apple as they do to the movement of rockets or planets in space.

nova A faint binary star that suddenly flares up and becomes thousands of times brighter, then gradually fades and becomes dim again. Astronomers think that matter is attracted from one star, builds up on the other star, and then explodes, making it look as if a bright new star has suddenly appeared in the night sky. Nova means "new."

orbit The path of one body in space around another body in space. For example, the path of a planet around the sun is called its orbit.

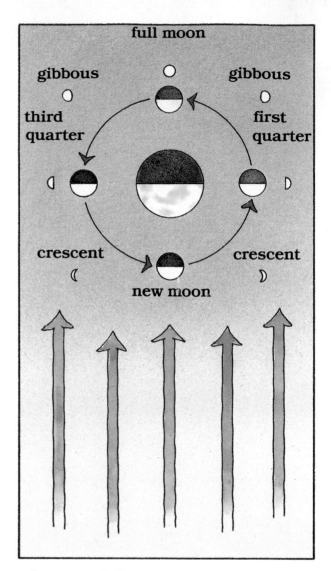

outer planets The planets beyond Mars: Jupiter, Saturn, Uranus, Neptune, and Pluto. Jupiter, Saturn, Uranus, and Neptune are giant planets made mostly of gases.

parsec A unit used to measure great distances in space. One parsec is equal to 3.26 light years.

phases of the moon The changes we see in the moon's shape as it orbits Earth. This depends on how much of the lighted half of the moon we can see. The four main phases are new moon, first quarter, full moon, and third quarter. A thin slice of the moon is called a crescent moon, and a thick slice (between a quarter moon and full moon) is called a gibbous moon.

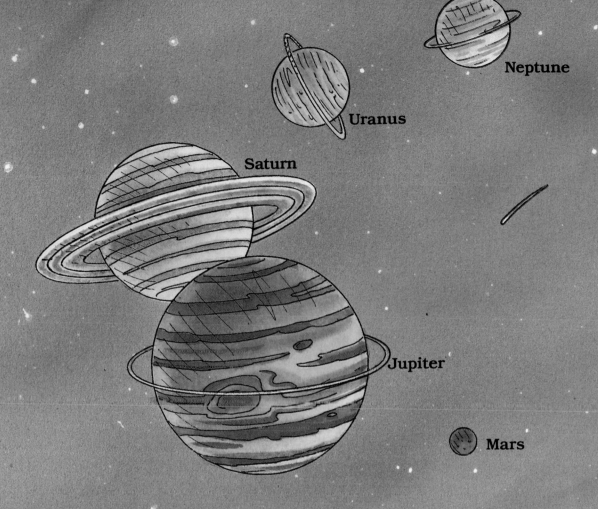

Pluto

Neptune

Uranus

Saturn

Jupiter

Mars

Earth

planet Any of the nine large bodies in space that revolve around the sun. In order from the sun, the planets are: Mercury, Venus, Earth, Mars, Jupiter, Saturn, Uranus, Neptune, and Pluto. A planet does not give off light as the stars do, but shines by the reflected light of the sun. Other stars may have planets of their own.

Venus

Mercury

pulsar An object that gives off a steady, rotating beam of radio waves, X rays, or visible light rays. It is thought to be a rapidly spinning neutron star. We receive a pulse of electromagnetic radiation each time the beam sweeps past Earth. The pulsar in the Crab Nebula flashes thirty times a second.

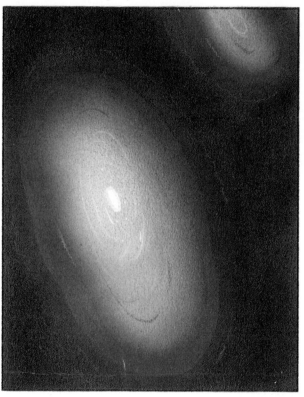

Pluto The planet that is usually the most distant from the sun. Pluto is now within the orbit of Neptune. In 1999 it will again be the most distant planet. It takes Pluto about 248 Earth years to make one trip around the sun. It is the smallest planet, less than 18 thousand miles (3 thousand kilometers) across. In 1978 astronomers discovered a moon of Pluto and named it Charon.

quasar A powerful source of energy within a very distant galaxy. Even though quasars may be thousands of times smaller than entire galaxies, they may give off hundreds of times as much energy. Some astronomers think a quasar contains a black hole 100 million times as massive as the sun.

radio astronomy The branch of astronomy that studies the electromagnetic radiation in the form of radio waves that comes from objects in outer space. The use of radio astronomy has led to the discovery of quasars, pulsars, and galaxies more distant than any previously known.

red giant

our sun

red giant A huge, cool star in a late stage of its life cycle when it has used up most of its nuclear fuel. Some red giant stars are 100 times bigger than our sun. Several billion years from now, our sun will become a red giant star.

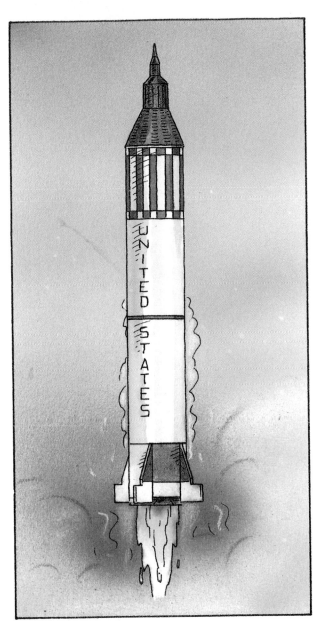

rocket An engine that carries fuel and the oxygen needed to burn the fuel. Because rockets do not need the oxygen of the atmosphere, they can travel in outer space. The hot gases escaping from one end of a rocket thrust the rocket in the opposite direction.

satellite An object in space that revolves around a planet. The moon is a natural satellite of Earth. A space station is an artificial satellite of Earth.

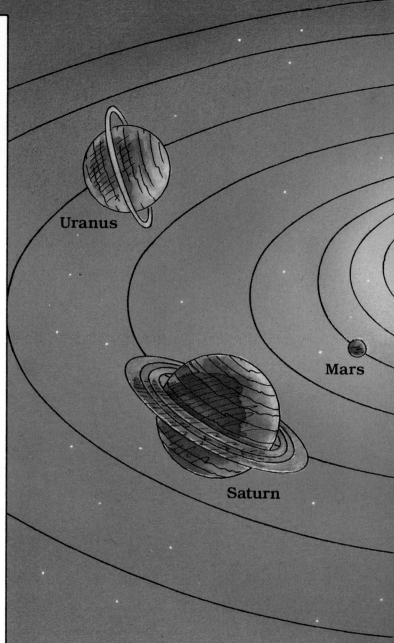

Uranus

Mars

Saturn

Saturn　The second-largest planet and the sixth from the sun. Saturn is about 169 thousand miles (272 thousand kilometers) across and orbits the sun once every 29.5 Earth years, at an average distance of 887 million miles (1,430 million kilometers). Saturn is encircled by a beautiful system of rings that are made up of tiny pieces of ice.

shooting stars　*See* meteors

solar system　The sun and the family of nine known planets, more than 50 moons, and millions of asteroids, comets, and meteoroids that revolve around it. Despite the presence of all these objects, most of the solar system is empty space.

Sun

Mercury

Earth

Venus

Jupiter

Neptune

Pluto

space Everything beyond Earth's atmosphere.

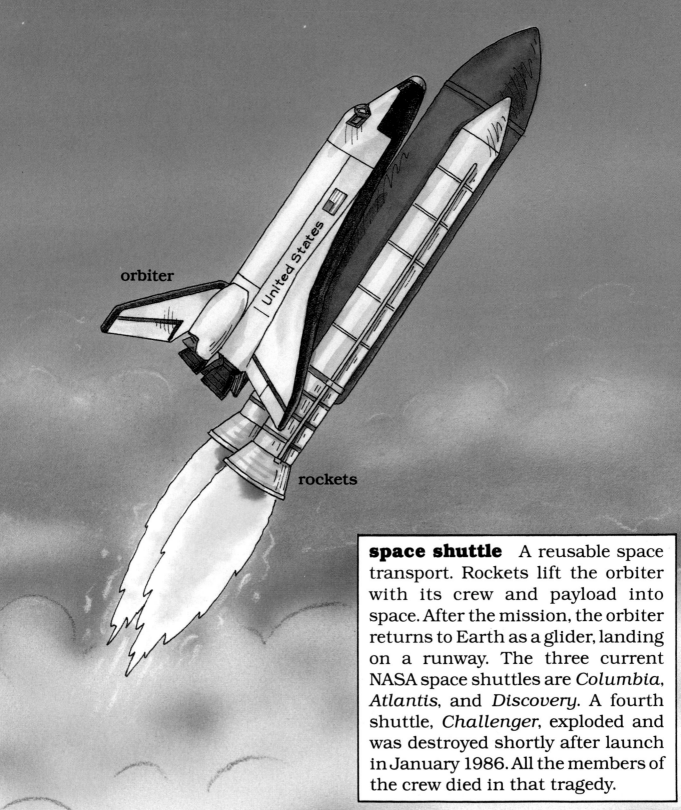

orbiter

rockets

space shuttle A reusable space transport. Rockets lift the orbiter with its crew and payload into space. After the mission, the orbiter returns to Earth as a glider, landing on a runway. The three current NASA space shuttles are *Columbia*, *Atlantis*, and *Discovery*. A fourth shuttle, *Challenger*, exploded and was destroyed shortly after launch in January 1986. All the members of the crew died in that tragedy.

space station A large spacecraft in a long-lasting orbit. Astronauts work for long periods inside the station. The first United States space station, *Skylab*, was occupied by three crews during 1973 and 1974. The Soviet space station *Mir* was launched in February 1986.

space suit A protective garment worn by astronauts. Space suits provide air pressure and oxygen to keep the astronauts alive. They also offer protection against extremes of cold and heat and harmful radiation.

star An object in space like the sun that gives off its own light and other kinds of energy. Stars make energy by means of nuclear fusion. Nuclear fusion occurs when the nuclei (the center parts) of atoms are joined together and make heavier atoms. This results in the release of huge amounts of energy.

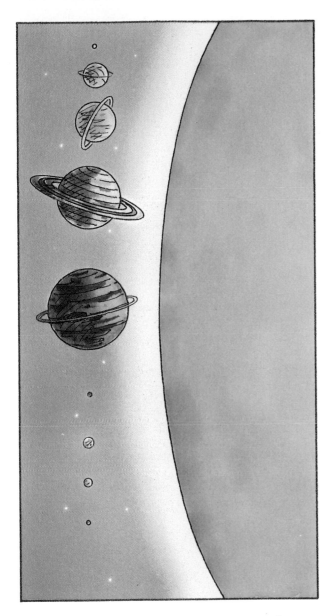

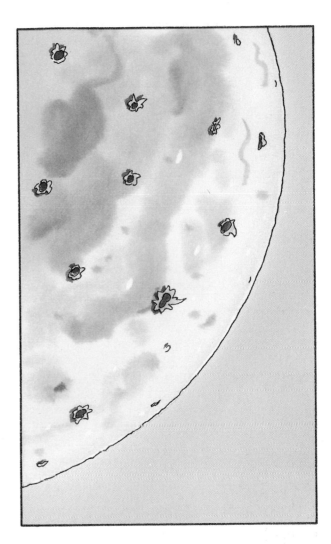

sun Our star, the center of our solar system. The sun is about 865 thousand miles (one million three hundred ninety thousand kilometers) across and is on average about 93 million miles (149 million kilometers) from Earth. The sun is 600 times bigger than all the planets put together.

sunspot A dark region on the sun's surface associated with strong magnetic fields. Sunspots are slightly cooler and much darker than surrounding areas.

supernova A giant star that suddenly explodes and for a short time becomes millions of times brighter than the sun. In February 1987, a supernova flared up in a nearby galaxy called the Large Magellanic Cloud.

space telescope in orbit

ground observatory

telescope An instrument consisting of a combination of lenses, or mirrors and lenses, that is used to gather and focus light in order to view distant objects in space. Astronomers use telescopes to study stars, planets, and other celestial objects.

universe All of space. Everything that exists in the natural world.

Uranus The seventh planet from the sun. It was discovered with a telescope by William Herschel in 1781. Uranus is a gas giant about 30 thousand miles (49 thousand kilometers) across and is on average about 1,783 million miles (2,870 million kilometers) from the sun. Uranus has at least 15 moons and a system of thin rings.

Venus The second planet from the sun and the one that comes nearest to Earth. A close twin to Earth in size, Venus is about 7,545 miles (12,140 kilometers) across. Venus is covered by dense clouds, and its surface temperature is hot enough to melt a metal like lead. Venus is the brightest planet in the sky. It is often seen in the early morning or the early evening.

Voyager 1

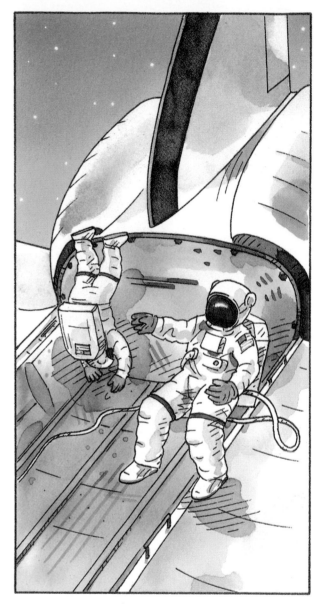

Voyager 1 and 2 United States space probes that were launched in 1977 to explore the outer planets. Both _Voyager 1_ and _Voyager 2_ visited Jupiter and Saturn between 1979 and 1981. _Voyager 2_ then visited Uranus in 1986 and Neptune in 1989. Both _Voyager_s have passed beyond the nine planets of our solar system and will someday be lost in outer space.

zero gravity A term for the weightlessness that astronauts in orbit experience. The term is misleading because gravity is always present, even in orbit.

zodiac A circular band in the sky around which the sun, moon, and planets appear to move.